Fierce, Fearless

&

Flawed

Flairs and Glairs

Publication House

"Fierce, Fearless & Flawed"

ISBN No: " 978-93-90416-24-0"
1st Edition
Language – English and Hindi

Flairs and Glairs
Publication House
Regd. Under MSME Act.

Disclaimer

This is a work of fiction and solely represent the thoughts of the corresponding authors of the articles. Our editors have tried their best to edit the content of all the authors and check the plagiarism.
All the write-ups in this book are unique and are only published in this book.
In case any plagiarism or error is found, only the author is responsible alone, and not the publisher or the Compilers.

Cover Designing and Book Formatting
Shubham Shah and Ishani Agarwal

Acknowledgement

The completion of this undertaking could not have been possible without the participation and assistance of so many people whose names may not all be enumerated. Gratitude towards all the co-authors, those have toiled hard to make this book to be successful one.

We are thankful to Flairs And Glairs publication, without whom, this project would never have been possible. Moreover heartfelt thanks to our parents, family, relatives and friends for their continuous support and encouragement towards us in completing this book. Above all to the Great, Almighty, the author of knowledge and wisdom, for his countless love.

Co Authors

Shubham Shah (Founder Flairs and Glairs)
Ishani Agarwal (Co-Founder Flairs and Glairs)

1) Jyoti Matania (Compiler)
2) Lipsa Sahoo (Compiler)
3) Sattarupa Pandit
4) Rajesh Kumar Sahoo
5) Jayanti Kumari Jha
6) Smita Kumari
7) Bhagyashree Das
8) Sarah Mishra
9) Dibyani Senapati
10) Shreya Srivastava
11) Priyanka Ojha
12) Manish Matania
13) Ria Matania
14) Krutika Satish Ghanekar
15) Sougam Ojha
16) Shibangini Debata
17) Priya B Singh
18) Barkha Matania
19) Anisha Das
20) Samra Maimoon Usmani
21) V. Rathika
22) Khushbu Agrawal
23) Aman Sharma
24) Meghna Chatterjee
25) Abhilash Rout
26) Samparnna Dalbehera
27) Illa Kanungo Mohapatra
28) Sanjib Chowdhury

29) Trupti Prabha Sahu
30) Showmen Talukdar
31) Kodma Kudada
32) Swagata Banerjee
33) Nithya Kanagaraj
34) Aradhana Mataniya
35) Induprakash Deo Pnadey
36) Shaikh Abdul Wasee
37) Prisha Jain
38) Shreeyanshi Sukla
39) Louispriya Jena
40) Dikila Ladingpa
41) Shweta Pragyan Rout
42) Shivanjali Srivastava

Shubham Shah

(Founder- Flairs and Glairs)

Shubham Shah, an entrepreneur at "Flairs & Glairs" a brand with dynamics in events organizing and cultural educational pan INDIA, is a 26yrs old guy who recently has entered the digital platform of imprinting emotions. He has initiated with

his own open mic platform to help budding poets and aspiring writers under his brand named as "Teekhe Zasbaaat"
He is a commerce graduate from the Bhagalpur City of Bihar.
He states Writing has impersonated him since childhood and he has now been writing for over a decade!
Cooking, on the other hand, is his passion! He also mentions, trying out new things just tickles him!
When asked sir, Why SPICY EMOTIONS?
He smiled and added, "agar jasbaat teekhe na ho toh wo jasbaat kahan" Spices are all that blends! So do his words!
As a chef, he presents to you his dish! Hot and freshly served! Taste it! Feel it! Enjoy it! You can also find his writing in the Book "Teekhe Zasbaaat" and 50+ Co-authored anthologies. With his passion to explore opportunities across Platforms, he is working with keen devotion and We wish him all the very best for his future ventures.
He is Featured in the **International Magazine De-Mode** for his upcoming solo novel.
He is **Approved by Ne8x for its Lit Fest,** and is a **Golden Star Awards 2020 Winner.**
He is an **India Book of Records Holder** for his Anthology **Satrang,** and has the **Grandmaster** title by **Asia Book of Records**, for the same.
He has also been featured in **Prabhat Khabar**, **Dainik Jagran** and other renowned Newspaper for his achievements.
He has also been awarded with **India Star Republic Award 2021.**
He has been a proud co-author to

India Book of Records (Title- Black)

World Book of Records (Title -15 Wonders of Poetries)

India Book of Records (Title - Aaina)
Vajra World Records Holder (Title - Gustakhi Maaf Hai)
High Range of Records Holder (Title - Gustakhi Maaf Hai)

Share your reviews on his

INSTAGRAM
@spicy_emotions
@shubham4shah

Or via email on
shubham2shah@gmail.com

To stay tuned to his work and opportunities follow his business Handles

INSTAGRAM FACEBOOK YOUTUBE

@flairsandglairs
@teekhezasbaaat

WEBSITE:
https://flairsandglairs.in/
https://flairsandglairs.com/

Ishani Agarwal

(Co-Founder- Flairs and Glairs)

Ishani Agarwal hails from the City of Joy, Kolkata.
She is the co-founder of her Community "Teekhe Zasbaaat" and Flairs and Glairs Publication.
Been a Compiler for 45+ Anthologies, she is in the process for more. Co-authored in 150+ Anthologies. She is a India Book of Records Holder, a Vajra World Records Holder, a High Range of Records Holder and a Bravo Record holder.

Approved by Ne8x for its Lit Fest 2020, and Literary Icon 2020. Also a Golden Star Awards Winner 2020.
She has also been awarded with India Star Republic Award 2021.
She has been featured by the National Magazine "Taree Zameen Par" with the title 'unstoppable'.
Also featured in the International Magazine DeMode for her upcoming solo novel, she is proud to write on social issues, and is happy with the love she is receiving.
Connect with her on Instagram: @Ishani_agarwal_quotes / @compilations_so_far

COMPILER
JYOTI MATANIA

Born and brought up in Odisha, Jyoti is currently pursuing her bachelor's degree in political science.. She wants to be a legacy, as of now writing has allowed to be ME!! Till date have co-authored in 15+anthlogies..A debator, fashionista; being the best version of myself....by being fierce fearless n flawed.

Celebrating yourself, the way you are has allowed her to pen her feelings, and be voice for voiceless...Uh can connect her on her insta handle @theroyal_mataniagirl

Will stand Out: Fierce Fearless &Flawed

"I love to see a young girl go out and grab the world by the lapels. Life's a bitch. You've got to go out and kick ass." answers Maya Angelou in the conference of women entrepreneurs, when a woman is said you don't know anything 'Better mind your household stuff!!'

Nothing could be truer for the women entrepreneurs who are chartering unknown territories unabashedly and fearlessly. Each one of them is scripting her own success story in today's new age world. Starting right from ecommerce, education, investing ,travel,fashion ,

retail ,fitness hiring and 'Anything and everything

under sun' they are proceeding with gumption and unbridled enthusiasm to change the world for them and around them. They are fighting across the world to make a difference with their ideas, seek solution that never have been sought,fight diseases and social norms, run successful ventures , generate employment for many and give rise to new

sustainable ecosystems. In the world we live today our identity is defined by our ability to be independent (and that comes from finance).

Should go ahead to launch a dynamic ecommerce business or lead a complacent life ahead??questions herself Falguni Nagar a mother of two and a fifty year old. She was a former MD of Kotak Mahindra Capital Company, but she choose to quit the job where everything was absolutely right emerging to become the successful beauty entrepreneur. 'I am building Nykaa to have a life of it's own.' -Falguni Nagar(Founder & CEO of Nykaa)

From trying to break free from the shackles of social discrimination, cultural bias,tags of being an inferior sex to fulfilling their responsibility of maintaining a home and a family woman finally have conquered.

It won't be wrong to say that "A woman can be both Mother and a Ceo"

CO-COMPILER
LIPSA SAHOO

She is Lipsa Sahoo, from Jajpur, Odisha. She is nineteen years old. Currently she is pursuing her graduation in English honors at Vyasanagar Autonomous College, Jajpur Road, Odisha. She started her writing career, just after the completion of her 12th Board examination. Writing is her passion and she aims to come across millions of hearts through this. Heartfelt thanks to her beloved father, for his continuous love, care and support towards her.
Instagram Handle: lipsa_sahoo.01

Women And Today's Society

Still today in this era of twenty first century, gender inequality is prevailing in the society. Our society is male-dominated one. In our society always a female is considered as a recessive one in each and every sector, starting from home to working sectors. The gender discrimination is marked since the birth of a girl child and continues throughout her life. She is biassed in each and every part of her life, starting from nutrition amount, quality of education to the choice of her marriage.

Today in this era of modernization, each female wants to be self-independent and self-sufficient. No woman of the present generation wants to beg for money for each and every small thing from their husbands. In order to fulfill their own needs, today females are studying hard by ignoring the gender inequality. Today females secure better marks than males and get well-settled jobs. Apart from this, the woman with less educational qualifications, strive hard to build up a small business to satisfy their own wishes.

On the daily basis, a female has to handle both, her family as well as her working sector simultaneously. She takes a lot of stress to keep everyone happy, her family members as well as her colleagues or customers. In the mean while she totally forgets about herself. Despite, her selfless care and struggle for everyone, each and everyone judges her.

In the process of being self-independent, women face a lot of challenges in their lives. The society abuses women for their frankness. Some females are tortured by their husbands at home, both mentally as well as physically. Moreover, many females are raped and murdered, just because they work for their self-sovereignty.

As we know that after every dark night, the beautiful sun rises, similarly a new dawn will surely arrive to our society one day. It's just because of the ugly mentality of the people that still today gender inequality prevails. It's the youth generation, who can surely bring a change in the society, in the near future.

PROJECT HEAD
MUSKAN SHAH

'I follow dreams to make them reality'
Muskan Shah, a girl from Jharsuguda, Odisha. Currently a Company Secretary Professional Student, and an Interior Designer.

A writer and a Poetess.
Being a writer she writes all genre : stories, articles, quotes, content's, etc. And being a poetess she writes poetries and they are her forte.
Her journey till date has been amazing by being a compiler of 10 Anthologies and a co-author of 50+ Anthologies.

A woman

A woman so bold
Fearless and strong
A woman has to be fierce
Because she is gold
She is beautiful
Not just in face but mind
She has a heart so pure
If you are one of a kind
Family, job, love or children's
She has the capability to manage all
She is an epitome of vitality
She is sometimes taken for granted by call
From being out to managing a house
She masters it all
She is amazing the way she is
Sometimes she is as cute as a doll
A woman defined by her father first
And later by her husband,
knows how to make a name of her own
Because she is a diamond
Believe her, she can,
She just need some support
Your trust can make or break her
Just be her supporter, be a sport.

SATTARUPA PANDIT

She is from Jajpur, Odisha. She is a nature lover. She love to travel and visit new places. Her hobby is to dance and paint. She is a good speaker and debater.

Promoting women entrepreneurship in India

There is a mantra in Yajurveda- Sa visvayuh sa vishvakarma sa vishvadhayah indrusya twa bhagam somen aatnachmi vishno havyam rakshya. Meaning she (lady/women) is the life of universe, She is the creator (Vishvakarma), She is one who holds all as a mother (vishvdhayah). She is the part of The one who has controlled senses (Indra-male), The one who is full of life (som-male), The one who could brought her up properly (Vishnu). As she is the solution, the medication.

According to Indian tradition, culture and scriptures, women are always given a special place in the society. They are considered to be goddess on earth. The word women evokes amongst things like grace, affluence, abundance, auspiciousness and authority. She is the one who had a galaxy in her eyes and universe in her mind. They have been regarded as a symbol of spirituality in our scriptures. She may not be physically as strong as men but her mental strength gives her the capability to change everything and built anything.

As per Joseph A. Schumpeter, Entrepreneur is one who innovates, raises money and assembles inputs and chooses mangers and sets the commercial organization going with his ability to identify them and opportunities which other are not able to identify and is able to fulfill such economic opportunities."

All the qualities that are required to be a successful entrepreneur are somewhat hidden in women. They are visionary thinkers. They can look outside the box. They perceive the world in terms of what it is not rather than what it is. They stick with a thing long enough to see results. Women can utilize their experiences and soft skill aptitude with emotional intelligence for properly leading their companies. The modern world women has been able to overcome the hurdle of societies perception of considering them to the confined to the four walls of the house or viewing them as weak entrepreneurs caught up in limited business areas.

There are thousands of opportunities for women to start their career as entrepreneurs. In history there are no less examples of women to admire who have succeeded as entrepreneur and proved their hidden entrepreneurial potential. Kiran Mazumdar Shaw, the founder of Biocon Limited is known as India's wealthiest self-made woman who found a biopharmaceutical firm in 1978. Falguni Nayar, the Founder of Nayka has become very famous among Indian women. The company offers more than 850 brands and has introduced 35 physical stores,

The government also encourages women entrepreneurship in rural as well as urban areas .Various women cooperatives schemes has launched by central as well as state government to help women in agro-based industries (like dairy farming, poultry farming, animal husbandary, horticulture, etc) as well as other small bid businesses. Several NGO's and other voluntary organizations support women entrepreneur financially as well as morally. Even training programmes have been organized by government as well as non government organizations to train interested women who willing to join such small bid businesses. There are many more ladies to inspire women as entrepreneur. It is rightly said that- "A women is like a tea bag, you never know how strong it is until its in hot water. The motivations for becoming an entrepreneur are diverse and can include the potential for financial reward, the pursuit of personal values and interests, and the interest in social change. Women entrepreneurship must be molded properly with entrepreneurial traits and skills to meet the changes in trends, challenges in global markets and also be competent enough to sustain and strive for excellence in the entrepreneurial arena.

RAJESH KUMAR SAHOO

He is a resident of Bhubaneswar from Odisha. He have completed his studies in Forestry. Currently he is working as forestry professional. He love writing, music, art, yummy foods and travelling

She is best

She is nature, She is mother
She deserves all the respect
She is friend ,She is sister
She is God's beautiful creation and She is best.

She is teacher, She is daughter
Daughter loves their parents unconditionally even after their marriage.
But society exploits the women hood always

She loves and keeps her commitment
She works hard to get the achievement
She protects family values always
Still a man cannot offer her that loyalty which she deserves

She is the creation for spreading Love
She is stronger than male
She is having more patience
This world will be collapsed without her presence

Girl power

In the era of male dominance
She has shown her true power
In a society of fake promises
She has shown always love shower

Society tries to exploit her always
Exploit in the name of "Trust"
Still she stands strong in this storm
Even if she face cheat and worst

She is truly an inspiration to all
She never asks justice even after torture
Facing the cruel world is really tough
Still She is beautiful creation of God

Salute to girl power!!!!

JAYANTI KUMARI JHA

Her name is Jayanti Kumari Jha. She is recently pursuing her bachelor's degree in commerce. She lives in District Jajpur, Odisha. She always have been a kind of girl who believes in destiny. Some of her hobbies are reading, playing badminton, listening music, writings and travelling. She enjoys participating in various competitions like Debate, Quiz, Speech, Sports, Writings as well have been awarded in few of them.

She believes in simplicity not stupidity. According to her A girl should be like a butterfly pretty to see and hard to catch. Being real and unique is the priceless thing which can never be at sale.

Fly And Fly, Unless You Stop

"Expect the unexpected and whenever
Possible, be the unexpected".

"A successful woman is one who can build a firm foundation with the bricks others have thrown at her", a well said statement about those who had always dreamt of success in their life of struggles. As we are very aware of the fact that a talk on woman empowerment is always a topic of discussion in our country. Many have thoughts regarding women that they are very sensitive, emotional and mentally weak but they have always made it in their own way by becoming a better version of their own. They have excelled in every fields like social, economic, E-COMMERCE, business and many others.

At the same time every woman entrepreneur faces different problems on their way of promoting business such as gender discrimination, difficulty in acquiring funds, work family interference, lack of social support and regarding them as inferior and incapable. In spite of such hindrances they never get demotivated and stop their greed for success because "When you become fearless, the world becomes limitless". With the supporting line for this statement I would like to mention some very known names, "Jaya Jha founder of Instascribe and Pothi, Suchi Mukherjee founder of Limeroad, Falguni Nayar CEO of Nykaa, Tara Gentile who is top entrepreneur at Creative Live. Nearly 57% of these women started out solo.

It is truly said that "The hand that rocks the cradle rules the world". Literally it means that a woman maintains a balance in her life's schedule as she moulds the personality of her child as a mother doctor, teacher and a good mentor as well as does well in her professional life.

Over the past years, Leading conglomerates are appointing female CEOs and today there are more women running

fortune 500 business than any time in the past. The single reason of every successful entrepreneur is her confidence that she wears because "Confidence has no competition". So the need of the hour is not to empower only woman entrepreneur but every single woman to rise and shine as bright as gold with the tears of happiness in her eyes because:

When women are educated, they educate a generation

When women are respected, they become sunshine in life of many

When women are independent, they create stairs of success for others

When women are empowered, they nurture the society in a better way

Lastly, every woman should be Fierce, Fearless And Flawed because " YOU will be defined not just by what you achieve, But by how you survive". So FLY AND FLY UNLESS YOU STOP.

SMITA KUMARI

Her name is Smita Kumari. She is a school student. She resides in Jajpur, Odisha. She is a girl with desires to touch the sky. She likes reading books and exploring new ideas of my own. Her hobby is her passion, which is writing. She enjoy singing, dancing and debating. Her inspiration is her grandmaa. She is always in search of pure soul of her own as well as do something good for the society.

IF SHE WILL,SHE CAN

"Behind every successful woman is a tribe of other successful women,who have her back".Memorizing the time of early 80's and today we been seeing a great rise of women empowerment,in every field of life,from housewife to home minister,from chef to chieftain,from tailor to entreprenuer.

"Women are the largest untapped reservoir in the world.so think of when women will start discovering their own talent,then they can bring modification to the society,because its the woman who makes society. Women have justified their role as a daughter,sister,wife,mother and surely an entreprenuer.

If she can play a number of roles smoothly,then promoting bussiness is not a big thing for her.women had to overcome a lot of obstacles to reach the height of success.she has various responsibilities on her and she also looks after every nessecity of her family. When woman step out of her house and wants to discover her talent ,there are many hurdles that complicates her way.lack of moral support,difficulties in arrangement of capital,insufficiency of raw material, stiff compition ,limited mobility.

One of the greatest example of women entreprenuer is KiranMazumdar Shaw,she is an indian billionaire entreprenuer.she is M.D of biocon limited.similarly like her there are other many women entreprenuer such as Ankita Gaba ,co -founder of social samosha.com. Falguni Nayar,she is the founder of Nykaa.com.Aditi Balbir ,founder of V resorts. She hae been recognized as Dell foundation's 200 most powerful entreprenuers in the world,2016.

This is journey of struggling woman to bussiness.

"If she tries, she can take risk,
If she risks, she will,
If she will, then she can..."

BHAGYASHREE DAS

Bhagyashree Das from Jajpur, Odisha. Presently she is pursuing her studies on integrated BEd in BSc. And beside this she is preparing for NEET also she is having strong desire to become a doctor. She love to pen down quotes and various thoughts regarding love, life, emotions, inspiration and so on. Music is a part of her life. She love to listen various songs, little bit adventurous. Lastly, she wanna say she strive to impress herself.

"When women are the advisor,the Lords of creation don't take the advice till they have persuaded themselves that it is just what they intended to do;then they act upon it & if it succeeds ,they give the weaker vessel half the credit of it;if fails,they generously give herself the whole."

A woman entrepreneur represents a vast untapped source of innovation,job creation & economic growth in the developing world.

Many studies indicate that women start business for fundamentally different reasons than their male counterparts.While men start business primarily for growth opportunities & profit potential,women most often found business in order to meet personal goals,such as gaining feelings of achievements & accomplishment.

In many instances ,women consider financial success as an external confirmation of their ability rather than as a primary goal or motivation to start a business,although millions of women entrepreneurs will grant that financial profitability is important in its own right.

The global evidences buttress that women have been performing exceedingly well in different spheres of activities like academics,politics,administration,social work and so on.Now they've started plunging into industry also and running their enterprises successfully.

Women have owned & operated business for decades,but they were not always recognized or given credit for their efforts.Women face greater obstacles in accessing credit,training,networks and information,as well as legal and policy constraints.

Women's entrepreneurship will increasingly matter for both business and development.While women still face obstacles to establishing and growing their businesses,the good news is that there are now a variety of documented successful approaches to promote women's access to finance,training and markets.Each market is unique,and women entrepreneurs' demands are not universal; instead ,they need customized solutions.

SARAH MISHRA

She is Sarah Mishra. She is a ninth grader. Writing is her all time passion.

Fierce, Fearless And Flawless

"Freedom cannot be achieved unless women have been emancipated from all forms of oppression." A line quoted by Nelson Mandela. Gender inequality still exists in India within the households, workplaces and in larger societies. In certain developing nations like India, gender inequality starts manifesting largely. Despite some progressive legislative measures in recent years, brought about to pressure from women rights movement; media and public campaigns, many women continue to experience discrimination and violence in their everyday lives. In recent years, lot of discrimination against people from North Eastern India has been reported. Many North Indian girls face discrimination; are refused living accommodations when they travel to urban areas to study and are subjected to racial slurs in reference to the appearance of their eyes. I've often heard people saying that boys are prestigious to the family whereas when a girl is born, they're either aborted or given certain boundaries and restrictions. Such steps can create a huge impact on a women's character.

The economic equality and empowerment of women represents an opportunity for the world… to eradicate hunger, achieve considerable economic progress and provide a better future for all. Gender prescribes how we should be, rather than recognizing how we are. Indian women are global leaders and have powerful voices in diverse fields but most women do not enjoy their rights due to deeply entrenched and partial views, norms and traditions. With the prevalence of gender discrimination and social norms and practices, girls get exposed to the possibility of child marriage, child abuse and sexual abuse. All this still prevails in nations like India. Women aren't considered significant in a society. Many of these manifestations will not change unless they're valued more. They're constantly judged by people; some because of

their looks; some because of their character; and some even for their color. I don't think any woman should have to change their character or looks because of such stereotypes. What should be changed is the mindset of people and their way of perseverance.

It is critical to enhance the value of women by investing and empowering them with education, life skills, sport facilities and advanced quality learning; especially in rural areas. Empowering girls requires focused investment and collaboration. Providing girls with services and safety education and skills they need in life can reduce the risks they face and enable them to fully develop and contribute to India's growth. Globally girls have larger survival rates at birth, are more likely to be developmentally on track but India is the only country where more girls die than boys. This needs to change. Changing the value of importance of girls should include men, women and boys. Only when the society's perception changes will the rights of girls be respected.

"To show zero tolerance to gender inequality and biases, I stand up, confront stereotypes and I loudly say "YES" to a society that appreciates, respects and promotes human values."

DIBYANI SENAPATI

Dibyani Senapati is from Jajpur Road , Odisha.
Botany Student.
Age - 19 yrs.
Always believes in Hardwork.
Love to write quotes on Life.
Passionate writer and Dancer.
Traveling and Observing the world gives happiness to her.

Expecting the Unexpected: Women Entrepreneurs.

Women entrepreneur may be defined as a women or group of women who initiate, organize and run a business enterprise. Women entrepreneur is a person who accepts challenging role to meet her personal needs and become economically independent. A strong desire to do something positive is an inbuilt quality of entrepreneurial women, who is capable of contributing values in both family and social life.

Entrepreneurship is not just confined to any one gender now rather due to multi-faceted economic pressures women have turned up and realized that the survival of their families and their own potential lies only in working side by side with men. Entrepreneurship has been globally felt as a development and progressive idea for business world.

The Government of India has defined women entrepreneurship based on women participation in equity and employment of a business enterprise Women have owned and operated business for decades but they were not always recognized or given credits for their efforts . Often women entrepreneurship were invisible as they worked side by side with their husbands and many only stepped into visible leadership position when their husbands died. But a variety of factors have combined in recent years to contribute to the visibility and number of women who start their own business . According to U.S . department of labor statistics, female participation in the workforce was than 40% in 1960 but is predicted to reach 62% by the year 2015. As women enter the workforce in even greater numbers , they gain professional experience and managerial skills , both necessary to be a successful entrepreneurs.

Contribution Of Women Entrepreneur :-

1) Economic Contribution

a) Capital Formation - Entrepreneurs mobilize the idle savings of the public through the issue of industrial securities . Investments of public savings in industry results in productive utilisation of national resources. The rate of capital formation increases, which is essential for rapid economic growth.

b) Generation of employment - Women entrepreneur in India are playing an important role in generating employment both directly and indirectly . By setting up small case industries they offer jobs to people.

2) Social Contribution

a) Balanced Regional Development - Women entrepreneurs In India to remove regional disparities in economic development. They setup industries in backward areas to avail of the resources concessions and subsidies offered by government.

b)Innovation - Entrepreneurs have contributed many innovations in developing new products and in the existing products and services .All these have resulted in economic development by way of generating employment, more income etc .

c) Other contributions- Women entrepreneurs are the main actresses in changing the culture of society. In our country women are workaholics and participate outside the house and develop the since of independence and the like.

Thus women entrepreneurs in our country are directly and indirectly playing an important role in environmental projection, backward and forward integration and are acting as charge agents, thus contributing to the ecomonic growth of the country.

SHREYA SRIVASTAVA

She is from Jajpur, Odisha. She is studying in +3 1st year in Vyasanagar Autonomous College. Interested in debates, speech, essay etc.

"Beauty with brain"

Who stands up for whom? Who looks up for whom? At that very moment when this 'who' encounters with a human tendency of helping others or an art of living And this 'whom' get filled with a heavy sense of responsibility or a moral duty .Then, by erasing all distances and differences people come forward to lend their kind support instead of standing apart. Instead of teasing, trolling and mocking one another they begin to chase each other by following their footprints on the sand of time, sand of emotions.

Beyond all nails and fails, all fields and scopes when this six lettered word 'WOMEN' comes before our sight we get so amazed, baffled and puzzled. Like Oh my gosh! This pretty young lady. She's charming. She's beautiful. A HOMEMAKER. She's a boss .She stands up for herself. She stands up for others. Like beautiful like boss...One more time Oh my gosh!

Apart from all the facts and fantasies, it's really pretty to help someone with all our heart by not being self-seeking and single minded.

Our small efforts will make highlighted differences in the society as well as in someone's life. It would give them name, fame, identity, efficiency, food and shelter. It will bring smiles and shines on their faces.

No matter in whatever phase of life the needed person is trapped, will get wings and things to come up and achieve.

Truly said - "When two strong women support each other incredible things happen". Women Entrepreneurs hold the quality to make and break someone. By doing partnerships with small business women they can help them out financially and emotionally to a great extent. This business bond will allow them to touch new heights of success and victory.

Women Entrepreneurs are highly empowered and motivated and can even bring the small business ladies in joy, passion, inspiration every single day .

"One and one makes two and sometimes eleven too". In that sense women can get a better chance to enhance their skills and occupy a better and revered standard in the society. It would eliminate gender based discrimination prevailing in and around them at a higher rate.

Usually , to meet and manage the demands of the family women step out of the doors and involving themselves in small businesses is one of the finest thing among the other alternatives. They opt for the businesses like pickles, embroideries, making and baking etc. So, if a strong business woman get interested and make up her mind to do some great deeds and provide a better opportunity to new talents and fresh ideas. Then, we can pronounce the needy women as enough fortunate. It would be brilliant for both, the one who helped to promote small businesses and the one who is being helped. It will make one happy and the other happiest. It would welcome new hopes and aspirations. Together their business will get success, power and will be boosted up. It would make each one of them more self- served, self-reliant, inspired, devoted, dedicated and flawless .

All of them will 'BLOSSOM'.

PRIYANKA OJHA

She is Priyanka Ojha of class IX studying in St. Mary's School, Jajpur Road, Jajpur, Odisha

Women can also be tycoon if given a chance.

In today's modern era, the contribution of both sexes is very important for the development of our country socially, economically and culturally, but, this is not reflected in the present scenario. There was a time when women were not allowed to step out of the house, or carry out her own business, etc. But, with the demands of situation, the mindset of people has gradually changed a lot. With the advancement of time, women have also stepped into the business world.

Nowadays, people want to give the best to their children and family which is not possible with only men's income. Thus, apart from being a mother, wife, etc. and supporting family socially and culturally, women have also started to support their families financially by establishing small cottage industries. From being a small businesswoman selling pappads to as big as being the chairman of large scale industries, women entrepreneurs have left such footprints which not only inspire other women but also adds into the country's economy. Cottage industries or small scale industries are mostly preferred as they can be done sitting at homes which is a big benefit for women. They can do their work while tending their families. These type of industries need little or no money to get started with which makes them the best option for the entrepreneurs.There are many women who stand as bright examples as entrepreneurs. One of them is Indira Nooyi – She is a Indian-Amerian businesswoman who is the chairman and Chief Executive Officer of PepsiCo.On 14 December 2013, she was awarded by the President of India Pranab Mukherjee at the Rashtrapati Bhavan. Inspired from such entrepreneurs woman have started small cottage industries selling many products like handkerchiefs, masks, food items, crafts, clothes, etc.

But, they face many difficulties too. For example, women need loans for buying raw materials and marketing their finished products. In such difficult times, government schemes come as a rescue for the entrepreneurs. They start many schemes and projects for financial support, transportation, raw materials, etc. Some of the schemes are :-

1. Mission Shakti

Mission Shakti started by Odisha Government is one of the successful programmes of the Naveen Patnaik government since 2001. So far under the programme around 70 lakh rural women have been successfully organized.

2.Mudra Yojana Scheme

This is a general government scheme for women who want to kickstart their entrepreneurial journey on a small scale such as, beauty parlour, tuition centre, tailoring unit, etc.

3. Bhartiya Mahila Business Bank Loan

Bhartiya Mahila Business Bank Loan's focus is to provide financial assistance to underprivileged women. Women under this scheme can avail loan up to Rs 20 crores which are to be repaid in seven years.

4. Cent Kalyani Scheme

Women business owners who manage MSMEs or are involved in agricultural work or engage in retail trading can avail loan under this scheme.

5. Udyogini Scheme

Women entrepreneurs involved in agriculture, retail and similar small businesses between the ages 18-45, whose family's annual income is less than Rs 45,000 are eligible to avail up to Rs 1 Lakh. The main advantage of the Udyogini Scheme is low-interest rates on business loans and no income limit for widowed, destitute or differently-abled women.

To sum up, a women, apart from serving her family and in-laws, have taken out time for creating and establishing their self-identity. They have made a distinct place for themselves in the society. In my opinion, they shouldn't be questioned.

Sometimes, even their own family members don’t support them.
I feel that we all should be pillars of strength for them because if one woman gains ground, many will follow her and in this way, India will rich a great height of success one day.

MANISH MATANIA

He is Manish Matania. He is currently working at a startup business. Expressing thoughts in writing is something he is always fond of. This book he feel is a huge platform for him

No one can stop her: Women

Yes, so it is in India women are, therefore, regarded as better half of society. In terms of Schumpeterian concept of innovative entrepreneurs, women who innovate, intimate or adopt a business activity are called "women entrepreneurs."Therefore, while writing on entrepreneurial development, it seems in the fitness of the context to know about the development of women entrepreneurs in the country.

In a nutshell women entrepreneurs are those women who think of a business enterprise, initiate it, organize and undertake the risks, handling economic uncertainty involved in running a business. Perhaps the risk factor that a woman carries, both indoors and outdoors, proves that she is proficient and competent enough to handle it. Women's desire to work at the place of residence, the difficulty of getting jobs in the public and private sectors and the desire for social recognition has made them at par with men. Our age old cultural traditions and taboos arresting the women within four walls of their houses have made their conditions more disadvantageous. Although the conditions seem unfavorable for her, she succeeds each time and I am reminded of Julie Andrews who says "Perseverance is failing nineteen times and succeeding the twentieth." With the growing awareness about a business and the spread of education among women over the period, women have engrossed themselves to 3 modern E's, Engineering, Electronics, Energy. The glimpses of women entrepreneurs manufacturing solar cookers in Gujarat, small foundaries in Maharashtra and T.V. capacitors in Odisha have proved beyond doubt that given the opportunities, they can excel their male counterparts. Several National and International organizations and agencies have appreciated the need and importance of developing women entrepreneurs in recent years, starting from United nations till Tirslldatiam Conference of Women entrepreneurs at New delhi.Inspite of all these when a women steps out to live life on her terms she is a subject of criticism. But then a strong woman believes that she is strong enough to face her journey, and a woman of faith believes that it is in this journey that she will get even stronger.

RIA MATANIA

Born and brought up in Odisha,
Aspiring to live life on her terms. Writing makes her HER!!
It helps express her core.
U can connect her thoughts on the insta handle matania_ria

Human being is the only species capable of shedding nature's reactive survival..and we should make use of it in the fullest possible way -- by being FIERCE FEARLESS and FLAWED.

By being fierce for ambitions, by mastering the fear and by celebrating your flaws.

And this context becomes very true when it comes to women..as enteurpreneurs as CEOs and etc. But along with it comes unacceptance.. unacceptance by family unacceptance by society and it's blamed to be against norms.But who sets these norms?And very importantly why do we need to fit into these norms?It's WE who set these norms and it's only We who can break them.

Women aspiring for business are the worst affected and the support towards her counts zero. But the best comes from the worst.All that's required is standing up for yourself,believe in self when noone else does.This belief is must when we step into a business world carrying within lots of criticisms and doubts.All we can do is chase our vision and work damn hard.When women are financially empowered, they can transform families communities and countries.

Initiatives like SWARA-voice of women,OKHAI etc have given life to these ideas and discussions and thoughts.They have brought results.Women should be rather survivors not victims.But there should not be a world where women survive..there should be a world where women thrive;thrive to live thrive to achieve. Nothing changes in a moment or a day.But the slightest efforts of every single step can make the world better Along with it, w e cannot ignore some of the very good initiatives of government, corporate sectors and surprisingly of individuals even. And about individuals, they say obstacles and failures are our companions in the journey of success. Life might shake us to the core but there's always a positivity. We need to figure it out and it may,we never know,turn out to be our greatest strength.Failure,it's not the

outcome..it is NOT trying.Fail Fail Fail and then rise like a phoenix.It takes courage to be successful. After all things worth having are worth waiting for!

KRUTIKA SATISH GHANEKAR

She, Krutika Satish Ghanekar, a student at V.E.S College of Arts, Science & Commerce, Chembur, Mumbai. Currently pursuing T.Y.B.Com & Company Secretary. She have keen interest in writings right from her college days. Writing is one of her hobbies which eventually helps her to express. In my spare time she loves to sketch, play instrument & listen music. She loves to explore herself through various new activities and writings. She is thankful to her family & friends for all time support and blessings.

Life- A Mystifying World

Life is an unsolved mystery,
Try to solve it in your own style !
One day, definitely you'll create a history.

Intense Passion

Someone's passion live,
Where else someone's may die.
But a true passionate person,
Never forgets to fly.

Real Freedom !

I feel free when,
My restrictions itself are restricted,
And allows me freedom.
My failure itself gets failed,
And makes me succeed.
My hopelessness itself loses its hope,
And gives me a hope.

SOUGAM OJHA

He is Sougam Ojha. He have just completed his masters in Biotechnology. Other than studies, he love to write. It helps him give voice to his thoughts and is a great sense of relaxation to him. It is like giving life to feelings .

No Country can ever flourish if it stifles the potential of its women and deprives itself of the contributions of half of its citizens. Lower participation of women impacting the economic growth in India. Constituting almost half of the population, their participation in entrepreneurship is less than a third ! Many of the women-owned businesses are largely unorganized and restricted to rural India with much limited growth opportunities. Hence, India's women as economic resources remain largely untapped.

While women are ambitious in India, it has been challenging for them to contribute significantly to the economy owing to several structural and social barriers existing in our country.

Terms of society, unconscious biases, unfavorable working condition lack of financial support and the list goes endless.

But should we be blaming only society and the people around? A women with a strong will to do can never be held back. She ought to fight by being fierce fearless and by accepting her flaws.

The strongest desire of her makes her fierce ready to fight all circumstances. Fearlessness which is not about the absence of fear, it is the mastery of fear. It's about getting up one more time than we fall down. Being flawed is in a way a blessing. That is something which you individually can celebrate. Being flawed in a certain way makes us stand different in the crowd. And, these have carried women through long and tough journey. Today, women as CEO'S and entrepreneurs are no more dreams or impossibilities. They have become facts. And as we know, facts are facts and won't change on account of your likes. Government and corporate sector policies have proved boon for such women.

However the country need to cover more ground for woman to break conventional barriers and rise in the currently male-dominated enterpreneurial ecosystem. There

is a still lot to be done. An initiation to say, could be to create a close, blended network of these institutions and bodies to work together to create a nurturing ecosystem that promotes and motivated them to leap forward.

SHIBANGINI DEBATA

She is Shibangini Debata. Honesty is the best policy, she believes!!!
She loves her family a lot.

Women entrepreneurs in developing countries

Women are generally perceived as homemakers with little to do with economy or commerce. The topic of women in entrepreneurship has been largely neglected with in the society in general. Not only have women lower participation rates in the entrepreneurship than men but they also generally choose to start and manage firms in different industries than men to do. The transition from homemakers to sophisticated business women is changing. In modern India more and more women are taking up entrepreneurial activity especially in small or medium scale enterprises. Women across India are showing an interest to be economically independent. They are willing to be inspired by role models like Indra Nooyi, cheif executive_pepsico. Or Ekta Kapoor, creative director of Balaji telefilms. The Indian women are no more treated as beautiful showpieces. They have carved a niche for themselves in the male dominated world. Indian women well manage both burden of work in household front and meeting the deadlines at the work place.

Gender equality and economic development go hand in hand. Though the entrepreneurial process is the same for men and women, there are however,in practice, many problem faced by women, which are different dimension and magnitudes, which prevents them from realizing their full potential as entrepreneurs. Women play a pivotal role in alleviating poverty through productive work that they are engaged in outside their home. Although increasing women's participation in small ane medium scale enterprise is among the developmental goals and targets to reduce poverty, improved family health and empower women's economic status.

Women's entrepreneurship deals with both the situation of women in society and the role of entrepreneurship in the same society.

Women entry into the business, or say, entrepreneurship is traced out as an extension of their kichen activities. Women in India plunged into business for both pull and push factors. Pull factors implybthe factor which encourage women to start occupation or venture with an urge to do something independently. Push factors refers to those factors which compel women take up their own business to tide over their economic difficulties and responsibilities. With growing awareness about a business and the spread of education among women over the period, women have started shifting from kitchen to engineering and electronics. Women entrepreneurs have the unique tendency to build and maintain long-term relationships. They have more effective communicational, organisational and networking skills than their male counterparts. Moreover their fiscally conservative approach reduces the risk of failure of their organisations.

A goldman Sachs report states," enabling women particularly as entrepreneurs, benefits future generations because women tend to spend more on their children's education and health, which should boost productivity as well."

Overall, more women entrepreneurs account for improved economic growth and stability within a country

PRIYA B SINGH

Priya B Singh is basically from Dewas, Madhya Pradesh. She is a Former Educationist, communication Trainer, Random Thoughts Writer & Avid Reader, Amateur of Nature, Wanderer, little philosopher, Deep Thinker, She believes in actions, not on words,
Her writing keeps her at ease,
She mostly write quotes on thoughts.
Instagram id- instant__thoughts_

"Women as Entrepreneurs promoting small bid business women."

Women, whenever we listen this word, get a picture around, a family figure person, weaker gender, a center figure who handles a family beautifully. Whatever you ask her, she would respond gracefully, she's always there for everyone but when it comes to think about her own self independency, there's no way around.

Actually since Ancient times, we Indian have a strong mentality about a women, we have always seen her as a mother, sister, wife & daughter but never as a working employee or a business women.

No doubt women manage house beautifully, they even do their each & every part of work flawlessly cause whatever they do, they give their cent percent. As compare to other genders, women come as a weaker, rather she's the strongest one, she just needs open minded people around who could support her & let her do what she actually wants to do to become financially independent.

Well if a woman works, it's a good sign & an indication of their financial liberty, but unlike men, it creates extra burden on them. Men have single duty of earning only.

Working women are doubly burdened, they deal with official duty & household chores

together, it becomes hectic, after almost 8 working hours, coming home, after being tired, cooking food for the family & serving them cause this is their main duty & earnings come later in the part of women.

As our country is male dominated, people can't watch women working shoulder to shoulder. They think women who stays home, are fully dependable and once they get financial independence, they would get their liberty of taking own actions, performing several tasks of their own choice. This can't be acceptable to the Men.

BARKHA MATANIA

Her name is Barkha Matania. Currently she is pursuing her studies of commerce. Besides it she love crafting, debating and writing, which allowed her to voice for the voiceless.

Voice For The Voiceless

"The thing women have yet to learn is nobody gives you power. You just take it."

Days are gone when women remained confined to within four walls of their homes and their immense strength and potential remained unrecognized and unaccounted for. The fact remains that the citadels of excellence in academic and politics are no longer the prerogatives of men. Entrepreneurship is the perspective which numerous women have in her .A huge change of tradition has fluctuated the desires for the life of women. In the land were we worship Goddess DURGA as "shakti" thousands of innocent girls are humiliated.

Today women have reached the moon and Mount Everest, but on Earth her situation is same."When man are oppressed its a tragedy. When women are oppressed its a tradition"WHY?? The national award winner ,the Hollywood actress Priyanka Chopra spoke about "Breaking the glass ceiling:chasing a dream".Not only was her speech itself about how women shouldn't be boxed in,it was also about how women should be perceived by the world in general. We shouldn't call women victims, we should call them survivors. From SAINA NEHWAL to KALPANA CHAWLA, from our 1st woman president PRATIBHA PATIL to business woman NAINA LAL KIDWANI females have left no sphere unturned to prove their worth and credibility to society. Her thought "she believed she could,so she did"came right.

You can tell the condition of a nation by looking at the status of women. For me:"The question isn't who is going to let me, its who is going to stop me."

Women should be FIERCE, FEARLESS and FLAWED..

ANISHA DAS

She is Anisha Das. Currently she is pursuing her studies of science and have a great desire to be a doctor. Besides it, she loves cycling, comic reading.

The term 'entrepreneur' has been derived from the French word 'entrepreneur' means to undertake. The term entrepreneur may be defined as "an entrepreneur is a person who combines capital and labour for production". A "women entrepreneur" is any women who organised and manages any enterprise, especially a business usually with considerable initiative and risk.

Entrepreneurship is necessary to initiate the process of economic development of both developed and developing countries. It is also instrumental in sustaining the process of economic development. Every country tries to achieve economic development for prosperity and better life to people. So, contribution of both men and women is essential in economic activities for healthy nation building.

The challenges faced by women entrepreneurs are:- Non-availability of finance, production problem, lack of managerial skills, lack of knowledge, lack of education and awareness, mobility constraint, low level of risk taking attitude, competition from male entrepreneurs, socio-cultural disturbance, less confidence. The government has taken various steps for the progress of women entrepreneurship such as:- Women's Development Corporation (WDCs),Marketing of non-farm Products of Rural omenW, MAHIMA, Assistant to rural women in non farm development (ARVIND) schemes, Indira Mahila Yojana, Rajiv Gandhi Mahila Vikas pariyojana(RGMVP),etc.

Besides the challenges faced by women, they can become an asset for the society. for this they have to follow certain rules to be bold and fearless.

Belief in your unique. there is only one you. It's about who you really are, your values beliefs flaws makes you stand apart. So believe in your unique self.

Let your dreams fly. don't confine find your dreams in a cell. The universe is guiding you every day with opportunity is knocking your door but you got to understand the sign and grab the opportunity. So give your dreams wings and let them fly.

Be ambitious. There is absolutely nothing wrong in being ambitious set your goal and work bloody hard to achieve them.

Be greedy. Be hungry for ambition. It's ok if you want to have everything. You can have it all when you want it all full stuff as long as the grid is not harbouring anybody it's completely okay to want everything.

Do not compromise on your dreams. Fight for your dream. Don't leave to achieve somebody elses' bench mark. Set your own. Leave a legacy behind there is nobody who can tell you who you should be.

Fail fail and fail and rise like Phoenix.

One thing is certain like day and night is that you will fail and this doesn't matter. What matters is your action after the failure to spell your aside and move ahead. Also do not avoid failure always analyse it.

Be bold and take risk. you have to take calculator and educated risk to evolve. and then back them with your 100% effort and dedication.

You cannot please everyone. In the era of social media it's easy to be confused with people opinions. faces hiding behind anonymity and passing comments do not matter. Always remember that no matter what you do, someone will always be unhappy.

Don't take yourself too seriously. Appreciate the funny thing called love. There will be good times as well as bad times. So enjoy this roller coaster ride. Learn to laugh at yourself.

My mother always told me that there will be someone with whom will always be less fortunate than you. So give it back in any way to the society spread compassion and humanity.

Be a planner. it's good to have dreams. But it's even more important to have a plan and implement that the same if is effectively to achieve those dreams.

" So don't fill inside a glass slipper, when you can shelter the glass ceiling. "

SAMRA MAIMOON USMANI

Samra Maimoon Usmani is a teacher who loves writing and reading. She is an English Literature graduate from CALCUTTA UNIVERSITY and has completed her M. A last year. She is a passionate educator and dedicates her time to inspire students to perform well. She is a storyteller who delights in telling true stories of our society. She is writing from the age of 11 in both Hindi and English languages and continues doing so even now. Her articles are published in the esteemed dailies The Telegraph, Sanmarg and also on various online platforms. She dedicates her time in trying to delve deep in the problems of society and tries to create awareness to eradicate them.

MODERN WOMAN

I am a modern woman.
A woman who has brains.
I know what is wrong and right,
I know my boundaries and heights.

I have people who love me.
But their opinions are divided.
Some want me to fight,
Whereas others want me to be quite.

One wants me to brave all the pressure,
Other wants me to enjoy womanly pleasure.
They want me to rise and shine,
Whereas they want me to be divine.

Difference in opinions are there,
But it is because they fear;
They just want me to be happy,
As they know about society.

My parents taught me well.
On their teachings I dwell,
They taught me to love my culture;
And also to appreciate others.

I also have a loving lover,
Whose presence gives me power.
He is not a rich brat,
In fact he is a poor lad.

I am not with him for money,
But because his heart is not stony;
He gives me what I want,

Love,Intellect, Hope and his stand.

I have a mind of my own,
And it speaks in many tones.
Whether you like it or not;
Words will come out of my mouth.

You can abuse me at your best.
Even you can rape or molest.
But you can't hurt my dignity;
As you dont have the authority.

My modesty cannot be outraged,
And you cannot decide my destiny.
I solely have authority on me;
Whether it's my emotions,soul or body.

Because I am a Woman of today.
I am a Modern Woman.
I know when to say yes or no.
I am the Woman who knows

V. RATHIKA

V.Rathika is doing Master of Arts in English Literature. She is a Wattpad writer and a co-author of Christy Gnana Deepa's Anthology " Secluded Hearts." She loves Literature and her aim is to keep writing for the rest of her life.

Superwoman

I see the walking Super Mankind
With full of energy
Running errands in my house.

She is the boss of the house
Yet the most kind hearted person,
The best Human Resource Specialist
In this world.

She is the counsellor
For every members in our family
Even though she did not major in Psychology
She surpasses all Psychiatrist
In the world.

She is an excellent Chef
Bringing out varieties of dishes each day,
The aroma fills the entire street
When I smell it from the corner of the street
I rush home with my mouth watering all along.

She is exemplary in gardening
She nourishes
Both the plants and the children
Till they grow independently
Having enough strength
To face the world all alone.

She plays primary role as a teacher
In her house
Mentoring,teaching and guiding the family members
To follow the path of righteousness.

She works feverishly
For the upliftment of her family.
She is a good Doctor
Who knows basic necessities
To keep her Family members healthy.
She is the greatest Economist
In this world
To adjust and run her family successfully
Even in times of financial crisis.

What is she not?
She is an artist
To bring the colour of joy
In all her family members face.

What she can't do in this world?
She can earn and manage her family at a time.
She is the career guide
Not only for her children
But for everyone around her.

She is an unpaid labour
Who works selflessly
To create the next generation
Of this world
By being an iron pillar of the era.

Each mother in this world
Is irreplaceable in her children's lives.
She is the epitome of Goddesses
No need to empower
A mother, a woman!
She is born empowered!

KHUSHBU AGRAWAL

Khushbu is a twenty-year-old girl currently pursuing her graduation from a renowned college in Odisha. She is a peace-loving person and is good in public speaking. She aspires to become an IAS officer and serve her nation.

Opportunities for women has been increasing in this generation. Until ages it was believed that women are meant to be in kitchen only. They rarely had a chance to get proper education. But now women are stepping out of their homes to create a new identity for themselves. They can be seen setting trends in business, in corporate world and every field of life.

For their immense love for fashion we can notice them opening boutique or make up products line. Or housewives starting small scale business of pickles or Indian snacks are very common these days. The term MOMTREPRENEUR can be used for the moms who besides having the responsibility of a baby and family commitments, do business as another income and support family. The White Revolution started in India to make it self-dependent in milk production is an evident example to illustrate woman's involvement in the business world, in it the women of Gujrat played a major role to make Amul (dairy cooperative society) successful.

Falguni Nayar the founder of Nykaa (online cosmetics and wellness products company) is now inspiration for millions of women who think of starting their own company

The mindset of the people has also changed significantly. These days parent teach their daughters to be self-dependent and prepare for the worst. Partners being understanding and helping out in problems related to work. Indian govt has different schemes for working women and with its law has reserved some rights to empower them.

But now as the time has changed so are the problems. The thirst for body of some individuals has made it difficult for women to head back to work freely. And the mentality that "only men are supposed to" understand and carry out things related to stock market, taxes, or any other technical stuff has made it even worse. It should not come as surprise that

people are not ready to invest in start-ups owned by women entrepreneurs because they doubt their capability of handling business. Companies are not ready to hire women because they feel she cannot be a team player in long run for being a woman she has to start a family soon. But women can be seen smashing this patriarchy like a boss.

AMAN SHARMA

Aman Sharma is currently pursuing his Bachelor's in Maths Honours but he is most interested in expressing his thoughts through his writings. Having a very intellectual mind which has a deep desire to explore the truth and causes of life and it's dilemma. He is also a co-author in about 10 anthologies with Flairs and Glairs Publication. Let's see what he have for you today.

From both social and economic prospectives, it's wrong to underestimate women in business. In today's world women represent the largest market opportunity and control about 20 trillion dollar in annual spending. But when we talk about India, according to National Sample Survey Organisation (NSSO), only 14% of business estimates in India are being run by women entrepreneurs. The data also revealed that most of these women-run companies are small scale and about 79% of them are self-financed.

For every women entrepreneur, it is vital to be a person of mettle as well as metal. Women must be of strong intent and be decisive of the purpose of establishing her business - from the initial objective, to the execution layout, to the end goal. It is important to carve out a definitive roadmap - whether it is a purely passion-driven pet project or with a commercial perspective to it; whether to maintain it as a small-scale boutique business or future plans of growth and expansion. All these factors need to be addressed with crystal clarity, which would then form the foundation for the framework for their business.

Women are natural networkers as they are naturally expressive, great conversationalists and a pleasure to interact with. The definition of professional networking for women should not be restricted to mere "business-oriented" benefits, but also to expand the horizons of personal knowledge and growth. At the end of the day, your company rests on your shoulders and you are the one navigating it. Networking should be with the angle of knowledge and learning factor as well, and a peer-to- peer platform is an ideal setting for such a situation

Understanding the translation of turning a "passion" into a "profitable business": Women entrepreneurs often tend to perceive their business as an extension of their hobby/personal passion, not realising that it also needs to sustain itself and turn into a profitable one as it progresses.

There is certain amount of neglect in making it an actual profitable and scalable business. To address this, women must learn the basic knowledge on how to scale-up their business if they have a desire to drive it to greater heights.

HOW WOMEN ENTREPRENEURS CAN OVERCOME THESE CHALLENGES-

TIME MANAGEMENT: Women can start by allotting the right amount of time to all activities of the day, with a dedicated timeline for each. This checklist not only monitors the daily activity in an efficient manner but also serves as a motivating benchmark for accomplishing targets and can greatly impact your mental state of mind.

PRIORITISING WORK AND HOME: For women, prioritising is a prime factor. It is important that women assess each activity and rank their activities in terms of priority-at work as well as at home. Ask yourself the question "In the scheme of activities, which task is of utmost importance?" Once you have your activities chalked out, delegation and execution can get much smoother and quicker. In the end, it's all about aligning your priorities to reach a synergetic level.

BUILD A SUPPORT SYSTEM at home, work and beyond: One of the most essential arms in the arsenal of a women entrepreneurs is that of a support system. Without this, it is difficult to get through the rough patches of business. Women need a sounding board and positive energy to keep pushing them forward. Build a great support system at home, work and beyond..

MEGHNA CHATTERJEE

She is Meghna Chatterjee from Calcutta.
She is pursuing Sociology Honours from St. Xaviers College Kolkata.
She is a passionate writes who has worked as a co-author of several anthologies like My Success Ladder, Shine within You , Illusionary Yours , The dark Side of the moon and many more.
Mail her at:- meghna.chatterjee1999@gmail.com
Insta handle:-meghna Chatterjee

Looking at her little child who was sleeping peacefully Arati smiled a beam of radiance and satisfaction.

Gazing outside the window pane she took a nostalgic walk down the memory lane into the days of recurrent tortures and trauamas from her in laws for having a dark skin and a poor family background.

The man whom she loved with all her heart and soul also left on her body the vulgar touches of harrowing lust and the cruel marks of domestic violence for not being able to meet the dowry demands of their family.

Finally Arati being triumphant in her goal of coming out of that abode of malevolence went back to her parents with her five months old little angel.

And from there only she began her challenging journey of making and dispatching a variety of pickles from door to door.

Though she had exceptional culinary skills and a pleasant disposition of amicability and patience still in each and every step she had to face the ignorance and discouraging statements of neighbors, friends as well as from distant relatives.

Arati smirk a brim of irony as she recalled the eldest lady of her locality who once simply turned down her mouthwatering tamarind pickle for the lack of the tag of a well known brand now at the end of every meal can't sustain without Arati's magical mixture of lemon chilli.

"It won't be that hyegenic and safe"would comment another lady of her locality sneering at Arati's drool worthy mango pickle,but today that same lady refuses all international brands just to enjoy the marvel of Arati's sweet and tangy delight.

Arati now turned her glance from the window pane to the innumerable jars over the table- ready to be delivered for the next day.

Those jars stood shining and smiling as the ultimate trophies of her success thriving in exotic spices and tantalising aromas.

ABHILASH ROUT

Abhilash Rout is from Cuttack, Odisha.

He has completed his graduation in B.Com with Accounts Honours.

He is preparing for competitive exams too. He has been working for the welfare of working out for the weaker sections of the society.

Writing has been a part of expressing his feelings & his thoughts into words.

He is working in Odia film industry as an actor, story writer and assistant director.

His Instagram handle is @coolcapt_abhilash.

He has taken part in more than 140 anthologies which includes international anthologies too.

" Women Entrepreneurship "

Every human beings have got
equal opportunities and
responsibilities irrespective of
their caste, gender and nationality.
Women empowerment has started
to lead a powerful start towards the
development in the society and
aim towards a better experience
in the future and improved one.
Women entrepreneurship has the
better scope because many new
opportunities have just been started.
It doesn't really matter if the
enterpreneurship is done by a man or
a woman but what really matters is the
way we channelize the proper planning
of the business or how we look after
the welfare of the the employees and
how we treat them.
Everyone works for their bread and
butter so how well behaved we are,
whether we are looking at the janitor to
the managing director of our company.
This mindset will be highly respected and
mostly women follow this rule of
respecting every individuals correctly.
It's better we should always give chance to
all those persons who really want to help themselves.

SAMPARNNA DALBEHERA

She is Samparnna Dalbehera. A girl in an alley to express herself through her words. A strong believer of happy mind and happy soul. Constantly trying to merge Physics and literature. She has co-authored quite a few books and looking forward to write a book of her own.

Women: A creator And a destroyer

Women, the name itself carries gravity of its own. And the aura it carries and spreads, makes lives charmer and better. But, when it comes to women who are fierce, fearless and flaunts their flaws and ultimately evolves from the walls of society's self made ethics which states women needs to be behind the doors covering their faces with 'pallu'. They were not supposed to be supressed but deserves immense respect being born as a woman.

The Vedic Indian society had always treated women to be of equal status with men in all aspects of life. They were engaged in professions like teaching, agriculture, spinning and weaving of clothes, business, etc. They were also allowed to be a leader and rule. They were allowed to choose their man through 'swayambar'. Their personality weighs equal to that of men.

But as time grew, in the Medieval India, women were recognised as wives or mothers, not even daughters. If a daughter borns to a family, they were treated as omnious. Women were treated as servents who cooks, serves, do all households. She was given no rights and always remained under the guardianship of men. Men used to sidekick women.

But in today's Indian society, women has learnt to speak her rights. She came out of the four walls and proved herself to the society that she is no less than a man. She can do everything that a male can do. She is involved in small bid business, sponsorships, education, leaderships and many more. She has made her roots strong enough and stand no less than a man. Now a days we can go round to market or stores, we find the working women counts more than men. More and more women are involved in business and earning their livelihoods. They are evolving and becoming independent. The day is not far when we will see women ruling and reaching heights. Women will never subordinate men but will stand beside him, stronger than before.

ILLA KANUNGO MOHAPATRA

Educational qualification- M.A in English Literature

The blessings of God , her parents and her teachers, the support of her husband, family and some special friends always fills positive energy in her.
Dream...This word is very valuable to her
She love dreaming and she love living that dream too. She always believe in learning so she always try to learn something.
Always attracted by the beauty of literature, magic of kitchen and garden greens.
The greatest inspiration for her is her grandfather. The desire to read and write came because of him. She love reading books newspaper, love writing poems and small articles. She also wrote in various magazines.
Love to help people.

You are treasure trove of knowledge

Every step of life...
not easy for you ..
There are so many obstacles
in your way.... ll
There is always a test for you,
A new challenge
waiting for you all the time... ll

You have to solve ,
a new mathematics
in all your life.....ll
You have to be emotional
with all the
beauty of literature ... ll

You have to draw ,
a special geographical map
for your own life....ll
You have to decorate ,
a beautiful character
for the history......ll

Everyday, you build,
a new science
around you...ll
Everyday you search ,
a new knowledge
to be friends with time....ll

O woman,
You are the temple of knowledge....
You are the one who gave this whole world,
A treasure trove of knowledge ll

O woman, you can build

O woman,
Don't be surprised
If sometimes ,this society
does not understand you then.....

Understand yourself,
Understand your own strength...
How will this society understand you...?

Those who have lost,
The key to wisdom
How will they understand,
Your importance .....?

Those who have forgotten
The path of humanity
How will they do
Your respect ..... ?

O woman,
Remember...God has given you,
the power to create
Only you can build ...
yourself and this society ll

SANJIB CHOWDHURY

Sanjib Chowdhury (born 04 November) is an Indian author & psychologist. Dr. Chowdhury accomplished various professional degrees on medical and mind management studies. He started his career as an IT executive to move as cybersecurity expert, after a few years to pursue his passion to heal people against long term diseases, writing on physiology, Science and spirituality, nature survival architect, modern agriculture research and dog behavior experts.

Bristi, a mid-30s girl spent almost 15 years of marriage with just like a simple home-made lady. Her mind turns to do something when her husband moved to a different city for his new assignment. Since birth, she terrifies about dogs, but 2 years before - one fine evening one cute Labrador came to her life to adopt, which turns her mind to show empathy, love and compassionate of all dogs around her sense.

She chooses to engage herself by dedicating her time for animals - especially for dogs. Starting from supporting the social causes, treatments, adoptions, rescues & recently she started crèche services by caring for dogs at her home. She has taken numerous initiatives like doorstep to pick up dogs from owner's places, initial medical check-ups, basic grooming, diet checks, engaging them with her family members by playing, cuddling and even video interaction with the owner. This helps the dog never feels missing their own home. Sharing love, interact with them frequently by playing with gesture and object, helps growing their comfort level at the new places.

It's been observed & feedback received by her client that they are extremely satisfied by noticing good improvement of their health adopted new behaviors, noticed by the owner were immense happiness can't breakthrough.

She has now full time engaged and managed her key resources to support her growing business. She has been taken an initiative to expand the business which is expected to create some jobs in various cities in India.

In an interview, she told - entrepreneurship has not just been a career shift, but it has given a new meaning and purpose to my life. "I feel like I have had a rebirth and I am determined to make it count!"

TRUPTI PRABHA SAHU

She is Trupti Prabha Sahu daughter of Mr. Loknath Sahu & Mrs. Sanju lata Sahu, from Jeypore (Koraput). She is in 12th Standard. Heartfelt thanks her beloved mother, for her continuous efforts and supports towards her.

Today's Society for Women & the independence they wants or they have.

India is an independent country from 1947 but the women and girls of this country still not have indipendent. There are still some Rules & Restrictions to women and to the girls. The first & foremost issue that is facing by women in child marriages. It leads to the psychological, social, mental and physical issues for that young girl. Another problem is the acid attack. It is done with the intention of taking revenge on a girl by throwing acid. Rape is the one of the most significant issues that are faced by girls & women's in India. It destroys entire life of them. According to statistics, it is the most common crime is on a girl or women all over the world. In tribal area women are beaten to death after accused of practising witchcraft. It is one of the superstitions in India.

Domestic violence is one of the issues in India that women are facing. A women is Insulted or beaten by her husband and her relatives in the home. Next issue is the Dowry system until today, it is practising in India. One of the most prevalent issues is Sexual harassment. It is also includes touching women or girl publicly, teasing her. Honour killing is one of the issues that are faced by women in India. A girl will be killed for marrying against the wish of her parents and relatives. Female foeticide is another biggest issue. Family members will kill a girl child in the mothers Womb it is because they consider a girl is a a burden to them.

The Independence that need our girls & womens in today's society.

Independence is a powerful gift that a women can give to herself. It can lead her to each greater heights and achieve higher goals.... Being an independent women means you speak your mind. You call people out when they start misbehaving or disrespecting you. You exercise the power of

not letting them get away with it. We can see a scow and steady rise of women in all fields of Importance. Women of today are not just restricted to cooking and taking care of their house holds, they have to step out their comfort zones to create their own images in the outside world as well. This is in short can be termed as women empowerment. Women in the world are financially dependent on their husband but they have to depend on herself. A women who is capable of standing on her own feet and has an opinion of her own is a role-model and a source of inspiration for other woman in the society. She motivates others to stand tall with dignity and say no to violence. It is extremely important that every women become financially independent so that they never have to feel helpless in life.

SHOWMEN TALUKDAR

A Tutor by Profession and A Writer By Passion..
He Believe through writing people can heal themselves.
Through writing he try to express his emotions and feelings.
His thought process and how he see the world..
Through writing you can change other's perspectives and change the world and make it a better place to live..

Women as entrepreneurs, Promoting small bid business women..

Women as entrepreneurs.. Are you serious?? Are you kidding me? You must be joking right..
This is the concept of our society when we say or represent women as entrepreneur..
No.. Standing in the 21st century, some people react like this when they hear women as entrepreneurs.
If a woman wants to start a business then she has to start it by herself whereas a man starting a business can take money from his parents and other individuals..
Actually we as a society judge or want to see women as a homemaker and not as a businesswoman. In this era women are progressing equally working as a home maker and starting their small startup business and we can conclude that women as entrepreneurs are not a myth not right now..
If you look into the current scenario or even before the current scenario many women started small startup like cooking and reaching the food as home delivery.. Women are designing Clothes and selling them online... Women are selling sarees, bangles, jhumkas and other jewellery products online
If you look at the current situation you will see women are progressing faster then men in many ways.
Mini women are opening boutique store, making handicraft items and designing interior house decor with their ideas..
Many women have created their small business at home only.. Due to the pandemic many women have started baking cakes pastries and making chocolates at their home and delivering it to nearby locations.
Even many women have started making bottle arts and selling them at an affordable price..

If you take the example of Nita Ambani you can see her as a very well known women entrepreneurs in India I am from West Bengal if you see Keya Sheth, she is one of the known beautician from West Bengal..Known for having her exclusive store by her name 'Keya Seth's Exclusive' and ayurvedic cosmetics invented by her with the help of her husband. I guess support is also needed to make a woman as an entrepreneur..

Women as entrepreneur is not a myth at all.. Now we can see women shining like a bright star in the night sky.. So we should support women for depending upon themselves by starting small bid businesses as a way of earning money and later growing the business in the near future..

KODMA KUDADA

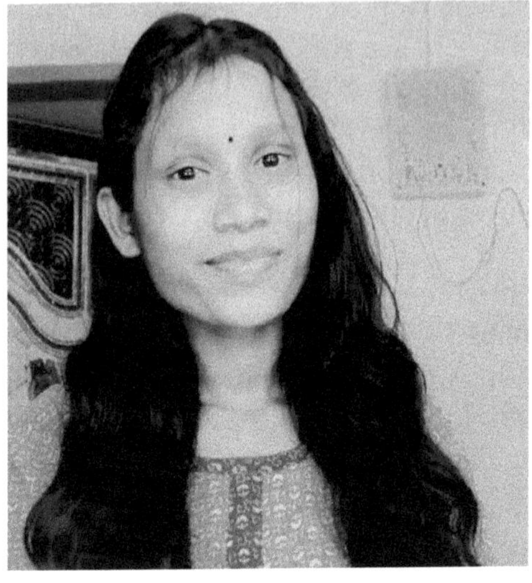

She is Kodma Kudada.
She believes that writing is life.

Women -The Supreme power

If a women can handle the accounts of home
She can also handle the accounts of business
If she knowns the like and dislike of the family member
She can also known the like and dislike of buyer
Cooking and mainting home is not her weakness
We make it weakness for them
If she can maintain the Whole house by herself
She can also maintain the business
We give wings to them for fly but if any difficult sitution happen with them
We take away their freedom and locked them in a cage
Stop doing this just teach and ready them to face it and again stand up
By taking selfies and celebrating mother's day and women's day that they feel special
You are wrong, if you really want to make her special just help her in making her journey of success

SWAGATA BANERJEE

Swagata aka Healer is an emotionally driven philanthropist, etching her way through the rational courses of life. She believes that simple joys of life begins with appreciating beauty in & out. Her writings tells stories of various shades of life and how they evolve through different scenarios. While being pragmatic in her approach, she tends to explore the optimistic angle of her tales.

A page from an entrepreneur diary

"veni vidi vici"-Julius Caesar

The incessant ring of her phone jerked up a rather sleep-deprived Priya. It's been two weeks since she had slept on her bed. She frantically searched for her phone through the files, printouts, cut-outs and what-not on her desk, and answered it absentmindedly, "Hello". On the other end was her best friend and business partner, Rita. As she held the phone, Rita pointed out that the meeting, for which they had been under crashing target for weeks now, has been rescheduled in an hour. Priya collected her thoughts and rushed to get herself ready for the meeting. While leaving, she looked at the mirror and saw herself, somehow she always felt a rush of feelings, butterflies you may say, within her, when she faced these meetings. It meant she has inched up a step ahead towards the dream of living her life on her terms. It meant…she lives her life…may be on edge…but that's how she likes it to be. She smiled at herself and said, "Good luck, beautiful" and left her office for the venue.

While she was in cab, her phone rang with a particular ringtone. She knew who it was, and smile curled up on her lips. This person had been inspiration and her call before every important meeting of her life, made her day. For her, she was her good luck charm, hearing her voice was that pixy dust she needed to create magic. She answered her phone, "Hello Daadi, had your tea?" On the other end she heard her chuckle. "So is my princess ready to shine?" she said. Priya said, "yes…I am". They had a talk, which came to an end with her reaching the meeting venue.

"Ladies & Gentlemen, Greetings!" Priya started her presentation of her organisation, The Furry Angels. Rita, herself and their band of girls has been working tirelessly for over two years to create this organisation what it has been today. They dream of making it a brand for organised pet

care business in India. " It gives me immense pleasure to invite you to be part of our journey…we are a team of 50 woman entrepreneurs....presently we have ninety pet care centres functional under our banner across the country…and we plan to be the face of pet care service business of India by 2030…" When she ended her presentation, there was silence for a few moment and then the spectators including panel members showered clapps incessantly. They were eager to be a part of the road map she had sketched, which meant she and her team were ready for the next lap of their race to make their dream a reality.

It was 9 P.M. Priya unlocked the door as silently as possible, but as she entered the living room, reading light was on. Her heart skipped a beat. She knew the next conversation. Her father looked above from his newspaper through his reading glasses and addressed her mom to re-heat the food. Once very close, she recently has spoken with her father quite less. Both of them have difference of opinion on her career choice and its anecdotes, and somehow silence has built the walls higher in between them. They had a silent meal, with intermittent small talks, and then she retired to her room and dozed off.

Next morning, her mother wakes her up. She goes to the dining table, and after a very many days sees her father smiling. She sits down pulling up a chair, her father hands her the tea and says with a twinkle in his eyes, "Have you read today's newspaper?" Priya takes the paper folded on the table by her side, and finds an article in praise of her work and yesterday's meeting on it. Suddenly, her eyes tears up, she looks up and finds happiness and pride brimming her parents' eyes. She knows she is ready, she is ready for the next stride.

NITHYA KANAGARAJ

Nithya, a left out part of a star, searching for every shimmering perfection in this wish-granting universe. She's been landed in profession as an engineer to cherish the future with technical rhymes. Cruising every second of life thanking those twinkling orbs through short stories, blogs, and artistic pieces.

Dive into my poetries at Instagram @the_poetic_quill_

HER

The slender shinning dot covered by the
The essence of night streaked lashes
Sorted out an algorithm
To maze out economic puzzles.
Those slim fingers pointed
Towards the beam of dawn
Taking out from indifference dusk
Larynx as soft as a flower petal
Lit fire to each
Inferiority complex souls.
Her every brave action
Converging to a point
Where the heart is brave
Enough to suck the imperfections
Of society and spread out
The fragrance of brilliance and wit.

PINK

A cute pink inquisitive soul wished for a dream. Giving chances to every other working is a good place. Made certain blueprints to pursue her career.

But, " No you're not allowed. Stay here.", a quite unfamiliar voice stopped her. "If a blue soul said like this, there won't be any barrels to pause him. This isn't the case for you, pink!"

Soon, she could able to see many disapprovals signaling her fellow mates from achieving their passion.

There held a gap between the masculine blue and the feminine pink. Those voices in the crowd said, "Only a man can do trade and reach goals. Step away from this path, you little flower."

The confused state of mind mourned to nature. "Are there any partitions among the wind, touching the sky? Do they need to specify their identity?"

On hearing the innocent's weeping, "Nope! Certainly not, dear. Those lines are drawn by mortals. It can't withstand in front of the power of nature.
YOU CAN BECOME WHAT YOU SEEK FOR!"

ARADHANA MATANIYA

Born and brought up in Varanasi,
She feel like writing completed her..
So far written 16 books for intellectual impairment children .She hopes to contribute in all possible ways to the growth of these children.

Female Entrepreneurship

Small and Medium Enterprises (SMEs) are of vital importance to the socio-economic growth of a country as they contribute to generation of employment, generation of income and poverty alleviation. The SME sector accounts for 95 per cent of all firms in both developed and developing countries1 and while they contribute to the Gross Domestic Product (GDP) of all countries, their value is of particular importance to developing countries with high levels of unemployment, poverty and income inequality.

Female labour force participation is important for an economy for many reasons. It indicates the utilization of labour in an economy (and in turn influences the growth potential); relates to income/poverty status; and acts as a signal of the economic empowerment of women. Fostering womens economic development through enterprise promotion can have a positive impact in a number of areas. It enhances economic growth and provides employment opportunities; in addition, it improves the social, educational and health status of women and their families as women invest more in education, health and well-being of the family. Despite all these possible benefits to the economy and the society as a whole, gender biases against women are common in the SME sector, a sector in which women should ideally be able to start up their careers as entrepreneurs. As the National Policy on Human Resource and Employment observes there is a gender bias in SME employment. Workers employed in SMEs are predominantly men. Good equal employment practices are needed to correct the above bias.

The general objective of this study is to examine the socio-economic and cultural barriers which hinder womens progression to SME sector. Furthermore, it would also look at the existing and future opportunities for women to enter and lead SMEs with a special focus on access and availability

of women - friendly Business Development Services (BDS) including development of business skills, technology transfer and linking with financial services. The study also aims to provide policy level recommendations to increase women entrepreneurs access to business development services and to identify national-level strategic priorities for stakeholders to work in economic justice with the aim of promoting women economic leadership and enterprise culture among women.

INDUPRAKASH DEO PANDEY

He is Induprakash Deopandey. He is from Jajpur, Odisha. He loves to sing, dance and read books

Women and entrepreneur

There are many more ladies to inspire as women entrepreneur.
A women is like a tea bag, you never know how strong it is until its in hot water. India is and had always been a hot and favorite destination for trade and business . with favorable climate ,affordable amenities and a huge amount of man power, India has become a hub for growing commerce day by day. And while it is prospering from business font , our Indian women stepped into it and gave it a new definition. The motivations for becoming an entrepreneur are diverse and can include the potential for financial reward, the pursuit of personal values and interests, and the interest in social change. ... Successful entrepreneurship often requires creativity and innovation in addressing a new opportunity or concern in a new way. the entrepreneur is an economic agent whose ultimate goal is to create a business from a well-defined project. To realize her project, she mobilizes a number of resources (knowledge-based, financial and relationship-based), from which she produces other resources (Employment,innovation, etc.)Women entrepreneurship must be molded properly with entrepreneurial traits and skills to meet the changes in trends, challenges global markets and also be competent enough to sustain and strive for excellence in the entrepreneurial arena.

SHAIKH ABDUL WESEE

He is Shaikh Abdul Wasee. Just a nobody trying to be a somebody. You can connect with him on @the_devoted_savage or @just_a_word_addict on instagram.

Honestly saying, before meeting her I never thought of a female as someone whom I would look upto after my mother. I was just...every regular boy of our country who thought that I am some superior authority over a lady or a girl whom I date or marry. But, she changed me. And not just with my mindset, but in ways I didn't even think I could have. She made me realise the actual reality of being a female in our society. People saw her as just a regular female who would just study and get married and any other stereotypical lady they want in an indian society. But she is, actually different. She plays cricket. And really, after meeting her I got the point when she made me realise what hardhsips you face being a rebel as a female and not as a male. We males walk at night like we own the city but females are either caged in the house or if they are outside, the constant fear keeps them conscious of the dark side of the society. She once said she had her menstrual cramps occuring, so I googled and gave her the hot water bag and ice creams and chocolates so that she doesn't feel that I am not there for her to which she said that what I did was very rare and unique which made me realise how faulty is the upbringing of males that we neglect their pain and suffering just by saying that it's natural. Now, some males will have a question that not all males are bad ? So my friend, why is it that every female has to be conscious of herself and surroundings while walking on the road ? Why is every female considered an omen in religious sites and rituals during her menstrual cycle ? She didn't just make me understand the bias they tolerate by being a female but also made me realise and helped me learn what it feels being a female in our society which holds males as an authority. She has and always been a person that I never want to lose in my life. I know many people must have written about accomplished women whom they see as their role model but I see her as my role model and I don't want to change that. She has shaped me in every

possible way and made me a better human being than I used to be. I wouldn't even be half a man if it weren't for her. And to everyone reading this, just spread this message and a vibe that no matter what your age, your status, your marital status, your official ranks or professional remarks are, you should never be ashamed being a female, or in general what you are and what lifestyle you choose. The very infinite beauty of being a female isn't in clothes or independence, but just being dignified of yourself not for just being a female but for being yourself.

.

PRISHA JAIN

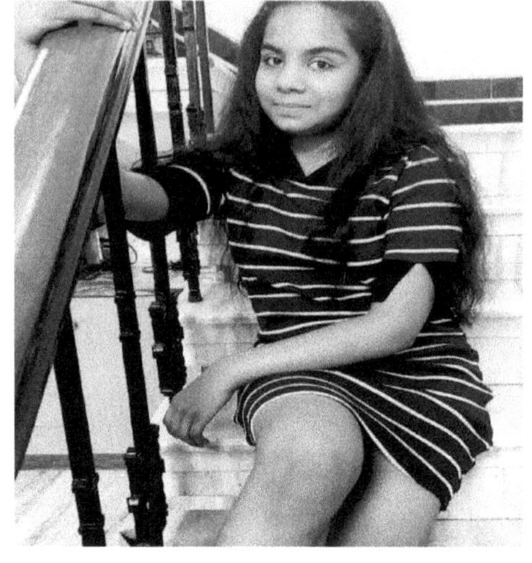

Name - Prisha Jain
Father's name - Mr.Anchal Jain
Mother’s name - Mrs. Karuna Jain
Education - Class 8
City - Indore
Hobbies - Dancing , reading , drawing , writing articles

DON'T DOUBT ON HER SKILLS !!

A woman is ambitious. In addition to supporting and encouraging you, pursuing your own goals and dreams, she will have her own as well .Her first and foremost objective is to take care of yours but her next goal is to earn money under her own steam .From a past few years each and every women have started doing small business of her own, it never mean that they are lacking financially, it is something they have initiated so that they can resume their passion and can nourish their skills. A well educated woman has full ability to be an entrepreneur, she can make good deals, more over she can appoint good employers for herself. Not only in India in the entire world woman are appeared as businesswomen and entrepreneur. A girl is not born for performing household chores and to not only supervise her family and children. From their teenage to their adulthood they are taught cooking and domestic work and are trained for becoming a HOUSE MAKER, but that is not the worry, the bothering thing is that when it comes to a girl's job the family at times become miser.

However the understanding and educated people have recognized a lady's worth of becoming pecuniary independent because of family's support a woman is transformed as entrepreneurs even after her marriage .women are running their own small business , taking financial risks . They are commonly seen as an innovator, a source of new ideas , goods and services . Existing Woman - Entrepreneurs are an ideal for the other girls (not only girls boys are also getting inspired by them) Actually this generation's Women are very much capable enough to hold up the circumstance and with that they are being perfect in every field known to a Man..This is tremendously Appreciable..it is the feeling of Proud for us , they are handling their both (family and work

) very nicely with full of happiness and they are doing ethical in both the cases, they take care and look after their Family in their leisure time and being as a mother also ruminate their children in their working hours too, After being so much tensed by the work a woman fulfill every demand of family and also have to do household work if they can't afford a maid .

Though being as a business Woman is not an easy task, there are some drawbacks of women who are Entrepreneurs, the society make fun of their hard work, Even they are taunted by the boys and old ladies..But they fight from a world , they definitely dodged a bullet .

Yet all Ladies who crave for moving out of the house and who desire to achieve the peak in their lives , are not espoused by the humanity , neither by the society nor by their own one .A woman is not asking to throw sympathy on them , they just want to gather your support nothing else , society should move ahead , its 21st century not 15th century..Boys n Girls are considered same, even girls are moving further than them , If a woman can handle house expenditures don't you think they can be applaudable in the business field. During this pandemic when individuals have lost their jobs, they were also economically depleting , from a Damsel to a Married Woman did not loss hope and started doing virtual-online work and they were merely successful .We should promote them to start their own business.

BE CONFIDENT ABOUT HER WORK , TRUST HER AND THEN SEE THE RESULTS ;).

"Don't doubt a woman
She is better than a man
She can be seen as an entrepreneurs
Every mission she will conquer".

SHREEYANSHI SUKLA

She Shreeyanshi,
She is in 10th grade.
She write quotes, poems, short stories, essays in her spare time in Hindi as well as English.

Whenever she says "I can", she hears an echo "you can't, try something else". And this something else includes tasks like washing dishes, nursing children and adults etc. which are not considered as work by our Ideal Human Society. And "you're talking of business? You don't have any idea about market, profits, losses, you have to deal with tough situations and you're not strong enough for that, it isn't as easy as relaxing in house all day". Yes, she can give birth to a baby, but that doesn't require any strength. She can solve everyone's problems, compromise with her happiness, but when does that prove that she's strong?

Nowadays, people's mindsets are changing. They are permitting us.... Yes, they are permitting us to start business, drive car, wear clothes of our choice. Wow! Isn't it great? We should celebrate this joy. Now we can do household works and get these opportunities. No matter whatever we do, we have to do the household works, because that's our duty. Everyone needs food, but cooking is only our duty, isn't it? I heard a man saying "yeah I permitted her to drive car", Now, I really wanna meet that woman, such a cultured woman. She did the right thing. Our constitution permits her, but without her husband's permission, constitution is NOTHING.

I think food is a basic necessity and have never read anywhere that earning food is a guilt for women. To earn food she can drive auto rickshaw, open a store, delivery food, open a tailoring shop, everything is okay. If you don't think so, you don't deserve to be called as a human. Because Nelson Mandela once quoted that "to deny people their human rights, is to challenge their humanity" and someone who challenges humanity is surely not a human. We don't want to depend on anyone for fulfillment of our necessities at least. After all everyone wants to feel the true essence of FREEDOM. If you can't encourage us, don't humiliate us.

LOUISPRIYA JENA

*Name - Louispriya Jena
*Class-10
*Hobby - Writing Article/short stories and reading Inspirational books

Women as entrepreneur, promoting small bid business women.

"Women" Women are the legends who gave birth to a man. But some of the men are very cruel against women and criticize women that "they are lady they can't do the work of a men....... " and more. But this is not true. A women can do whatever she want ,she has a right to live her life as her choice . No one can force her to live like their's rules and regulations. Society is totally agreed that "A women is borned to be a good mother, good wife, etc . She had no any works except house chores ".But why ?? Before, If a woman is widow then she can't get married again but a men can do that. Then how would she spent her life without her husband after getting married if she has no (especially newly married women).Some people also didn't want to have a girl child because they set up their mind to have a boy child as a man would work and get money to them. But why?? A girl is also that much capable of doing work .

We people also have listened that "Behind every successful man there is a hand of a woman". But those men were criticizing women.
But nowadays women are getting more successful than men in all sectors, they are also participating in all sectors.
Women help build an inspiring work culture by bringing in health competition, fastering teamwork, bonding and there by helping the company grow to its full potential.

Women are mostly seen working in hospitals because they have caring nature and they used to take care of their families. In education sector we can see women are mostly working and in leadership position. Because a woman can explain students properly and smoothly that some men can't

do properly (like angry with a student with bad marks, asking doubt many times, etc.).She has a patience to deal with students. Women's are tend to be a better customer service representative because they have excellent listening skills, patience, empathy, problem solving and telephonic skill. In most cases women are to be advertisers as they can represent a thing properly and attract customers towards the substances. They are also working as air hostess as they would behave respectfully and greatly with travellers and take care of them in the flight. Women are also working in defence lines, as a pilot, as an engineer, etc.

Nowadays women are not agreed to stay at home. They want freedom and wanted to do work for their self respect, some for their family survivable.

Long before women don't get chance to work as per their qualifications.But now for every work, seats are reserved for them.

Women are also setting up business in the hope of profit(by taking financial risk).Women who are not properly /highly educated are starting their own business like opening clothing stores, alterations shop, etc. Women are also driving(car,bus ,train, rickshaw, etc.) for their occupation or survival. Some are also working in the industries, groceries shop, etc. In most of the works women are getting a good leadership.

"Most women still need a room of their own, and the only way to find it may be outside their own house". These words are told by Virginia Woolf. Yes, these words are true because before, girls can't do jobs ,can marry another person after getting widow early, etc. But now she can do any work as her choice.

For these reasons now parents are wishing to Have a girl child.

In most of the cases women are the best option to be chosen up.

DIKILA LADINGPA

Dikila ladingpa from Sikkim, India. She has completed her Master's degree in Economics and currently pursuing B.ed. She believes purpose of life is living and living is learning and learning is enlighten implementing beside she is interested in writing,reading,exploring and travelling.

Get Inspire to Inspire

I had start my day with numb pain

Thinking it would gain some autonomous gain

From nowhere

having few pursuit that would refrain

My thoughts of losing gradually drag me insane

For the goals I desire

I stopped it there in the middle of nowhere

And walked a little while with tangled thoughts

Some responsibilities and unwanted restrictions held me back

Regardless I placed my hand on my heart crossed my finger
for the dream

And work that I had always admire

So I won't take a pause

For the goals I desire

I may not reach I may get tired I may fail

But I will keep on working until I reach my goal

My dust my dirt my drawbacks keep holding me tight

Pushing me hard like it's an ultimate fight

Yet I dropped down but I didn't stop

For the goals I desire

I kept walking into depth of despair

With symphony and mammoth fear

Hindrance won't leave the pace

Until I make the strong face

And tied up my champion's will lace

I live for now

I live it best

I may not be there where I am suppose to be

But I will work harder for where I need to be

Yes I am women

I get Inspire to Inspire

For the goal I desire

SHWETA PRAGYAN ROUT

Her name is Shweta Pragyan Rout. She is from Jajpur. She is 15 years old. She love writings because she use to feel a peace in it.

Women Entrepreneur

A woman means glory, a woman means beauty, a woman means blessings, a woman means nature, a woman which is a word, which can't be described just in words. They can create a world wi\th happiness, which is beyond of anyone's imagination. They can make a life or can destroy a life. Anyone can never pay for their work and love, it's priceless. They have never thought of profit in their love. They are just like a smile on a hopeless face. They are the gift of nature which has the power even to brighten a dark room. A woman faces challenges from her birth, she has no clue where and when her life is going to change. When she gets married, she have no idea about the family and the person to whom she gets married but still she sacrifices her whole life in their happiness. She never regrets in bad situations, as because she is always ready for it. She knows she can make everyone come out of the situation and can give a smile on everyone's face, even if she have to come out of the house and do job or business. She never takes back steps. Challenges are nothing for her, she knows that she is like a sun for many people, who need to be risen up to make the people wake up. There is no difference between the ancient and modern woman, ancient woman struggled for rights and today's woman struggles in their work. They try to do their best in both places because they want to make others happy. By doing her work, job or business she feels herself independent and introduce herself to the world. Never think that she is free of stress because she wears or eats nice. Even if she smiles in her stress because she don't want to give anyone stress. She faces new challenges every day. She has issues in her family and in her work. Sometimes she falls, cries but then she thinks that she can even make a source of water from that tears and this is what women are. She can make a way out of every bad situations. She can make a reason to smile from every situation.

Today a woman is free, she has her own freedom, her own independence, a new day and a new challenge in her work. She do it with a dream to be on top of the world. A dream for success, journey to introduce herself to the world. You can't even imagine her life. Every time when she falls, she comes back again with a beautiful heart and smile. A life with so much thing but still she smiles. Thry can never be compared to men, because they are greater than men.

SHIVANJALI SRIVASTAVA

Shivanjali Srivastava, just 20, a student doing BSc . She is from Lucknow (uttar pradesh). She believes that life is best gift from almighty we have received thus we should live it passionately.

She is writing not as professionally but following her passion and she thinks that "we write that only what we feel, what we observe from our surrounding." She also says that writing is the best way to pour-out oneself feeling or emotion than telling it .

She also loves to write short poems and quotes.

Instagram id: @ heartvoice_0403

To fly you need wings full of enthusiasm, and courage. To fly you need a mind full of openness, a heart filled with infusion, and a mind which trust oneself ability to fly high in the sky."

Having women in leadership positions can be in the company's best interest. Women constitute around half of the total world populationc. So is in India also. They are, therefore, regarded as the better half of the society. In traditional societies, they were confined to the four walls of houses performing household.

Most top and high power positions in business and companies are held by men, such as the case of Sweden. Women currently hold 4.4% of fortune 500 CEO roles, Research has shown " a consistent difference favoring men in accessibility to, and utility resources of power.

But in modern societies, women have come out of the four walls to participate in all sorts of activities. The globally evidences buttress that women have been performing exceedingly well in different spheres of activities like academic, politics, administration, social work and so on.

Now they have started plunging into industry also and running their ventures. As they have historically spent their lives creating families and building a home for them. These experiences help them generate workplace relationship.

But still to make themselves successful women, some of them have to face obstacle. At one time or another, most women who are CEO's of different companies find themselves in a male dominated industry or workplace that does not want to acknowledge their leadership role.

ALISON GUTTERMAN, CEO and president of JELMAR had this experience early in her carrier. "As a female entrepreneur in a male dominated industry, earning respect has been a struggle." She said.

Let us see about some wonder women, who had started as a entrepreneur, now earning million and have stood building and companies.

1. KIRAN MAZUMADAR - The founder of BICON LIMITED

She is known as India's wealthiest self-made woman who found biopharmaceutical firm market in 1978. This firm has entered in US Bio similar market and is getting the attention of investors. As per Forbes, it is the first company to get approval from USFDA. She ha put big fortune to build deep R&D- based biotech firm. In 2019 she held the title called India's 54th richest person and world's 65th powerful women. As far as her qualification is concerned, she did a bachelor's and master's degree from Bangalore University and Melbourne University respectively.

In next case, we are going to introduce another amazing woman, who has established an online business.

2. SUCHI MUKHERJEE- Founder and CEO OF Limeroad

In 2012, Suchi Mukherjee created online clothing and lifestyle accessories market place and named Limeroad. Today this company is known as India's most stylish online shopping website for men and women. She graduate in economics and went to economic school in London, to pursue a master's finance degree. If we talk about his achievement, she received many awards like Coolest start up of the year(from Business Today), Infocom wiman of the year- Digital business and Unicorn Start-up Award(NDTV).

WE have seen these women who have attained the height of being successful entrepreneur. Like this there is a queue of business women, who are inspiration for many young girls and also others women, to achieve something great.

MAYA ANGELOU says- "I love to see a young girl go out and grab the world by the lapels. Life's a bitch. You've got to go out and kick ass."

Nothing could be truer for the women entrepreneurs of today who are chartering unknown territories unabashedly and fearlessly. Each of them is scripting her own success story in today's new age world. Hats off to all of these women entrepreneurs.

At last I will end this writing with a quote :

"GIVE HER WINGS AND LET HER FLY.
DON'T LIMIT THE HEIGHTS OF SKY AND THE VERY NEXT MOMENT LOOK AT THE SHINE IN HER EYES.
SOMETHING MUCH BEAUTIFUL THAN THE STARS DAZZLING IN THE SKY.

Flairs and Glairs, a platform by a student for the students. We are esteemed youth struggling to carve out our path for our future and we follow a basic mindset Since everyone is not born with all-round skills. Joining hands with people who are born to execute it with perfection is the best way to evolve. Self-Evolution is the need of the hour but, evolving as a community is what we strive for. The initiative as kickstarted by, Founder- Mr. Shubham Shah with the motive to utilize the skillset and talent of writing has now a team of 10+ people who are actively participating into newer forms of learning and discovering talents among youngsters. We Provide platform and services like Publishing opportunities, Open mics, Workshops, Hands-on training. Operating with Brand Name of Flairs and Glairs (Publication House), we offer the chance of elevating a passionate writer to an esteemed author With Brand name Teekhe Zasbaaat. We bring to you an opportunity to get accustomed with the Public Speaking and Presenting of Thoughts along with regular challenges to brush up your inking spirit. The newest initiative to extend our services we introduced in a new writing Platform- The Glittering Fables and Ink Over Tears.

We Choose to Fly Like A Falcon than to be a Leg Pulling Crab.

To Know More: Infoline – 7781900870
Mail Us At-
flairsandglairs@gmail.com / info@flairsandglairs.in
Or Visit is at
www.flairsandglairs.com / www.flairsandglairs.in
Social Handles- @flairsandglairs @teekhezasbaaat

www.ingramcontent.com/pod-product-compliance
Ingram Content Group UK Ltd.
Pitfield, Milton Keynes, MK11 3LW, UK
UKHW022004190726
13853UKWH00004B/1730

9 789390 416240